K Is for Kissing a Cool Kangaroo

For Mary – G.A.

For Pam and John Hodgson, salt of the earth – G.P-R.

This book was originally published in Great Britain in 2002 by Orchard Books UK,
and in the United States in 2003 by Orchard Books.

ISBN-13: 978-0-439-53128-3
ISBN-10: 0-439-53128-4

12 11 10 9 8 7 6 5 4 3 2   9 10 11 12 13 14/0

Printed in the U.S.A.   40
First Bookshelf edition, December 2009

3 9082 11621 7277

K Is for Kissing a Cool Kangaroo

By Giles Andreae   Illustrated by Guy Parker-Rees

Scholastic Inc.
New York Toronto London Auckland
Sydney Mexico City New Delhi Hong Kong

Aa

a is for **apple** that grows on the tree

Bb

b is for **busy** and **big bumblebee**

Dd

d is for **dragonfly, daisy,** and **dream**

e is for **elephant**, mighty and strong

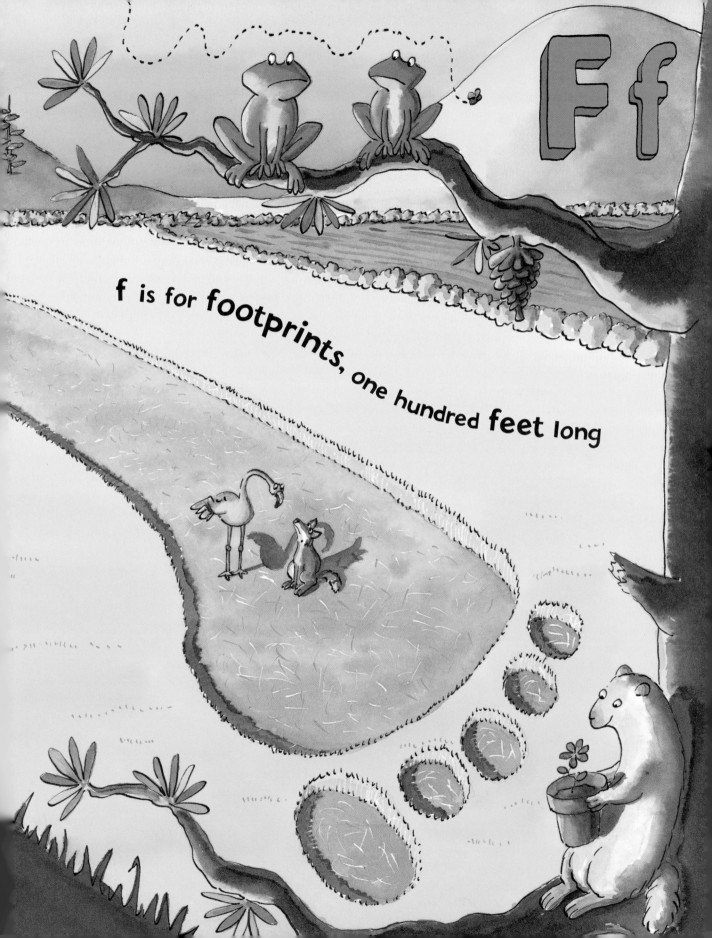

f is for **footprints**, one hundred **feet** long

Gg

g is for giant, whose garden grows wild

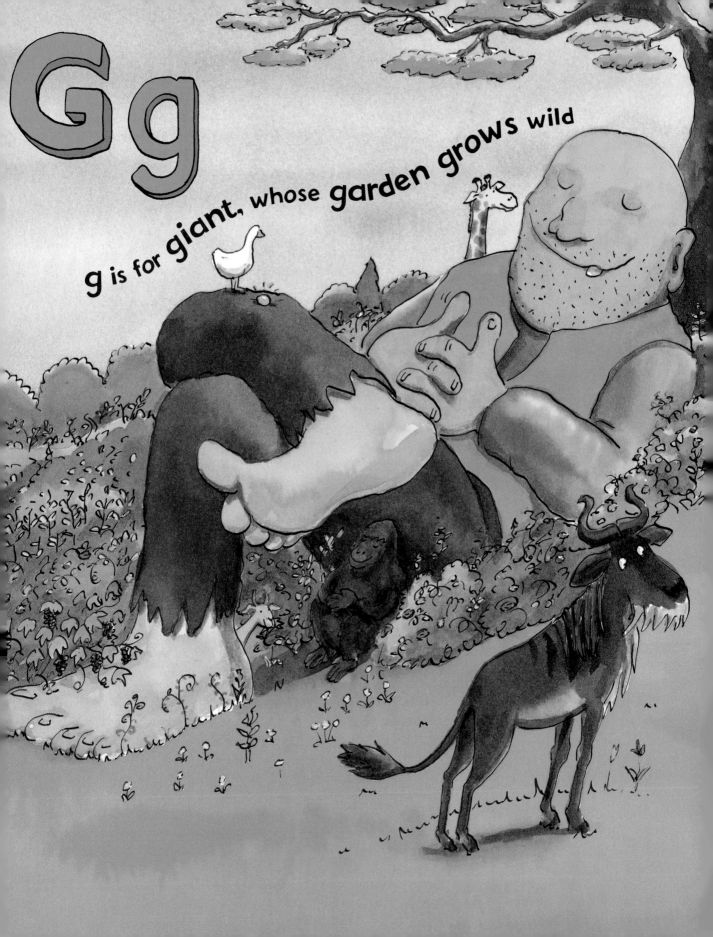

Hh

h is for **holding** the **hand** of a child

i is for **igloo**, a house made of **ice**

l is for **loving**, like Daddy **loves** you

m is for **mischievous monkey** and **mat**

n is for **naughty** and "**No**, don't do that!"

o is for **octopus**, arms everywhere

P is for **peaceful** and **piglet** and **pear**

q is for "Quickly, I've cuddled the **Queen!**"

r is for **robot** and **racing** machine

t is for **tea**time, so let's have some cake!

u is for **unicorn**, **uncle**, and **udder**

V is for **vampire** whose teeth make you shudder

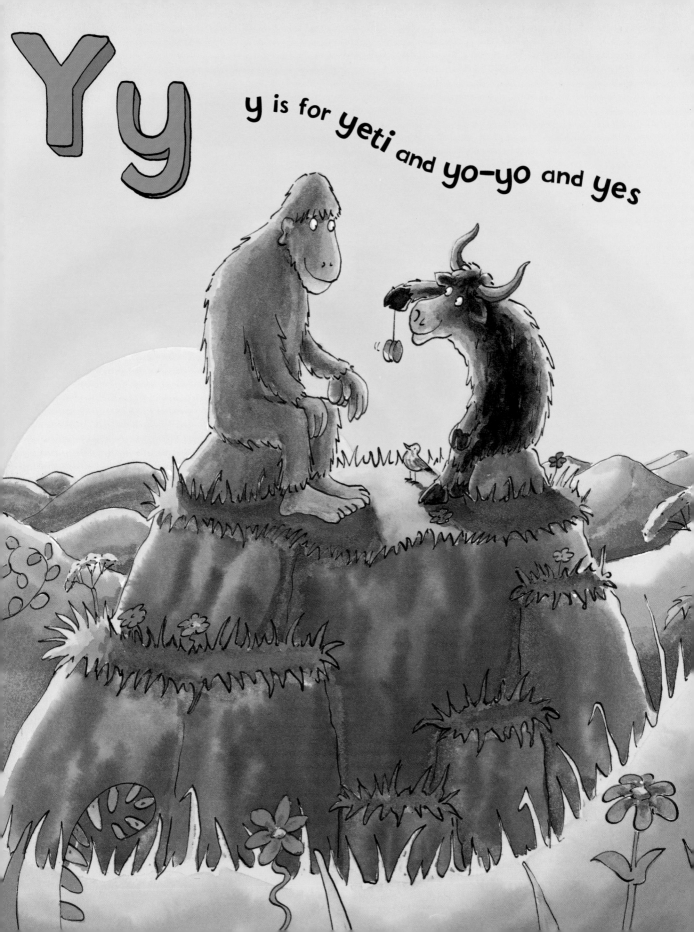

Yy   y is for **yeti** and **yo-yo** and **yes**

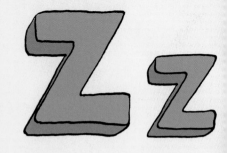

and **z** is for **zebra** – now how did you guess?!

On every page there are lots of other things you may have missed.

See if you can find them . . . then check them on this list!

Aa

armadillo

antelope

ant

bull

beetle

Bb

balloon

Cc

cake

caterpillar

clouds

dalmatian

dog

Dd

duck

Ee

emerald

emu

eagle

ferret

frog

Ff

flamingo

Gg

gnu

goat

giraffe

house

hamster

Hh

hyena

jester

Jj

jaguar

jam

Ii

icicle

iguana

ibis

llama

Ll

Kk

koala

ladybug

kitten

kiwi

lynx

Mm

milk

nectarine

Nn

newt

mole

mango

nest

pelican

Pp

Oo

olives

porcupine

owl

otter

pirate ship

Qq

quiche

quail

quack

raccoon

rose

Rr

rat

Ss

skunk

seal

salamander

toucan

Tt

teddy bear

turtle

Uu

umbrella

vulture

violet

Vv

vole

Ww

weasel

woodpecker

wombat

X ray

Xx

Yy

yak

Zz

zinnia